E
Ler   Lerner, Sharon
             Follow the monsters!

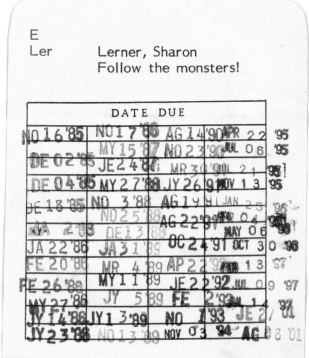

DATE DUE			
NO 16 '85	NO 17 '86	AG 14 '90	APR 22 '95
	MY 15 '87	NO 23 '90	JUL 06 '95
DE 02 '85	JE 24 '87	MR 30 '91	JUL 21 '95
DE 04 '85	MY 27 '88	JY 26 '91	NOV 13 '95
DE 18 '85	NO 3 '88	AG 19 '91	JAN 25 '96
	NO 25 '88	AG 22 '91	FEB 04 '96
JA 2 '86	DE 13 '88		MAY 06 '96
JA 22 '86	JA 31 '89	OC 24 '91	OCT 30 '96
FE 20 '86	MR 4 '89	AP 22 '92	FEB 13 '97
FE 26 '86	MY 11 '89	JE 22 '92	JUL 09 '97
MY 27 '86	JY 5 '89	FE 2 '93	JUL 14 '97
JY 14 '86	JY 13 '89	NO 1 '93	JE 27 '01
JY 23 '86	NO 13 '89	NOV 03 '94	AG 03 '01

A NOTE TO PARENTS

When your children are ready to step into reading, giving them the right books—and lots of them—is as crucial as giving them the right food to eat. **Step into Reading**™ **Books** present exciting stories or information reinforced with lively, colorful illustrations that make learning to read fun, satisfying, and worthwhile. They are priced so that acquiring an entire library of them is affordable. And they are beginning readers with an important difference—they're written on three levels.

Step 1 Books, with their very large type and extremely simple vocabulary, have been created for the very youngest readers. **Step 2 Books** are both longer and slightly more difficult. **Step 3 Books,** written to mid-second-grade reading levels, are for the child who has acquired even greater reading skills.

Children develop at different ages. **Step into Reading**™ **Books,** with their three levels of reading, are designed to help children become good—and interested—readers *faster.* The grade levels assigned to the three steps—preschool through grade 1 for Step 1, grades 1 through 3 for Step 2, and grades 2 and 3 for Step 3—are intended only as guides. Some children move through all three steps very rapidly; others climb the steps over a period of several years. These books will help your child step into reading in style!

Follow

Step into Reading™

the Monsters!

Featuring Jim Henson's Sesame Street Muppets

by Sharon Lerner

illustrated by Tom Cooke

A Step 1 Book

Random House/Children's Television Workshop

® Sesame Street and the Sesame Street sign are trademarks and service marks of the Children's Television Workshop. Published in the United States by Random House, Inc., New York, and simultaneously in Canada by Random House of Canada Limited, Toronto, in conjunction with the Children's Television Workshop.

Library of Congress Cataloging in Publication Data:
Lerner, Sharon. Follow the monsters! (A Step into reading book. A Step 1 book) SUMMARY: Rhymed text follows the adventures of a group of monsters on their way to Sesame Street. 1. Children's stories, American. [1. Stories in rhyme. 2. Puppets–Fiction. 3. Monsters–Fiction] I. Cooke, Tom, ill. II. Children's Television Workshop. III. Title. IV. Series. PZ8.3.L5493Fo 1985 [E] 84-18031 ISBN: 0-394-87126-X (trade); 0-394-97126-4 (lib. bdg.)

Manufactured in the United States of America 1 2 3 4 5 6 7 8 9 0

STEP INTO READING is a trademark of Random House, Inc.

Follow the monsters
wherever they go.

Sometimes they're fast . . .

sometimes they're slow.

Follow the green one,
the red,
and the blue.

Follow the old one,

8

the baby one too.

Follow them up.

Follow them down . . .

out of the country

and into the town.

13

Follow them out.

Follow them in.

Follow the tall one,
the fat,
and the thin.

Follow them high.

Follow them low.
Follow the monsters
wherever they go.

MONSTERS
AT WORK

Follow the monsters—
they all know the way—
all through the night . . .

and on into the day.

Stop with the monsters.
It's time to eat lunch.
They want a short rest
and something to munch.

Eat with the monsters.

A sandwich is great.

And then for dessert
eat your cup and your plate.

The monsters are tired.

But they do not care.

They're running.

They're racing.

They almost are there!

Fly with the monsters.

They must rest their feet.

Follow the monsters to . . .

Sesame Street!